For Mom and Dad
~ T.B.
For Chick and Babs
~ S.H.

LITTLE TIGER PRESS
An imprint of Magi Publications, London SW6 6AW
www.littletigerpress.com

First published in Great Britain 1999
This edition published 2003

Printed in Dubai
1 85430 926 9

1 3 5 7 9 10 8 6 4 2

THE GREAT GOAT CHASE

written by
Tony Bonning

illustrated by
Sally Hobson

LITTLE TIGER PRESS

Mr. Farmer had a field
and in this field he decided
to grow turnips.
So he ploughed the field and
sowed the seeds in long neat rows,
up and down, up and down,
until the whole field was done.

The seeds grew **and grew** and soon every row was filled with large, round, plump turnips.

Now Mr. Farmer had three goats
which he milked every morning.
But one day Mr. Farmer left the gate open . . .

. . . and the goats slipped through it, tripped
down the road and right into the turnip field.
They could hardly believe their good fortune.
Straight away, they began to chomp the turnips,
row after row after row.

Mr. Farmer, who was having a late
morning cup of tea, looked out of
his kitchen window and saw those
goats gobbling up his turnips.
"Oh no!" he wailed, running out of
the door, spilling tea everywhere.

Mr. Farmer then tried to chase the goats out of the field.
But those goats had minds of their own. One ran this way,
one ran that way and the third ran another.
Could Mr. Farmer get those goats out of the turnip field?

No, he couldn't!

"I know," said Mr. Farmer. "I'll get Dog."
He gave a loud whistle and Dog came running.
He rushed into the field and tried to herd the goats.
But Dog was a sheepdog and these were goats.
One went this way, one went that way and the third
went another, round and round the field until . . .

. . . Dog was exhausted.

Could Dog get those goats out of the turnip field?

No, he couldn't!

As Mr. Farmer and Dog stood at the gate,
wondering what to do, Horse stuck his
head over the fence.

"What's the matter?" he asked.

"Are those silly goats too fast for you?"

"Probably," said Mr. Farmer, wearily.

"Never mind, I've got good long legs,"
said Horse. "I'll soon have them
out of the turnip field."

Horse jumped the fence and raced up the field, sending turnips flying. Now Horse was bigger and faster than the goats, but they could turn more easily. One turned this way, and one turned that way and the third turned another way.

Could Horse get those
goats out of the turnip field?
No, he couldn't!

As Horse sat down beside Mr. Farmer and Dog,
Cow came up to them.
"Let me show you how it's done," she said.
"My big horns will soon send them on their way."

And so they did.
One goat went scampering this way,
one goat went scampering that way
and the third went scampering another —
every way but the right way.
Could Cow get those goats out of the
turnip field?
No, she couldn't!

Now Pig, who had been grinning at the efforts of his
friends, decided to show them how it was done.
"It's time to get tough," he said.
"Show them a bit
of muscle."

Pig pumped up his great shoulders and trotted into the turnip field. Then he dropped his head and charged with all his might. One goat nimbly tripped this way, one goat nimbly tripped that way and the third nimbly tripped another.

Could Pig frighten the goats out of the turnip field?

No, he couldn't!

Mr. Farmer, Dog, Horse, Cow and Pig all sat down
and cried their eyes out.
"Boohoo, boohoo, boohoo," they howled.
Just then, Little Busy Bee came buzzing by.

"What's the matter?" she asked. When they all told her, she said, "I'll get those goats out of the turnip field."
"You?" they exclaimed. "You? A teeny weeny, tiny winy, totty wotty, wee wee bee?"
"Yes me!" she said.

Mr. Farmer, Dog, Horse, Cow and Pig all stopped crying and began laughing and laughing until they were flat on their backs, legs-in-the-air hysterical. When they had finished splitting their sides, Little Busy Bee said, "Can I go and get the goats out of the turnip field now?" "All right, off you go!" they said, drying their eyes.

Little Busy Bee flew into the turnip field.
She buzzed round and round the goats'
heads, and then she said —

"IF YOU
DON'T LEAVE
THIS FIELD RIGHT NOW,
I'LL STING YOUR BOTTOMS!"

Could Little Busy Bee
get those goats out
of the turnip field?

YES, SHE COULD!

The goats didn't need a second
telling. As fast as their little hooves
could carry them they were off,
out of the gate, up the road
and on to the hillside.

At the gate Mr. Farmer, Dog, Horse,
Cow and Pig all stood, feeling very silly.
"Sorry, Little Busy Bee," they said humbly.
And they all agreed that sometimes
little folk can do things much better
than big folk.